Marie-Grace
AND THE ORPHANS

By SARAH MASTERS BUCKEY

ILLUSTRATIONS CHRISTINE KORNACKI

VIGNETTES CINDY SALANS ROSENHEIM

★ American Girl®

THE AMERICAN GIRLS

 1764 — KAYA, an adventurous Nez Perce girl whose deep love for horses and respect for nature nourish her spirit

 **1774** — FELICITY, a spunky, spritely colonial girl, full of energy and independence

 1824 — JOSEFINA, a Hispanic girl whose heart and hopes are as big as the New Mexico sky

 1853 — CÉCILE AND MARIE-GRACE, two girls whose friendship helps them—and New Orleans—survive terrible times

 1854 — KIRSTEN, a pioneer girl of strength and spirit who settles on the frontier

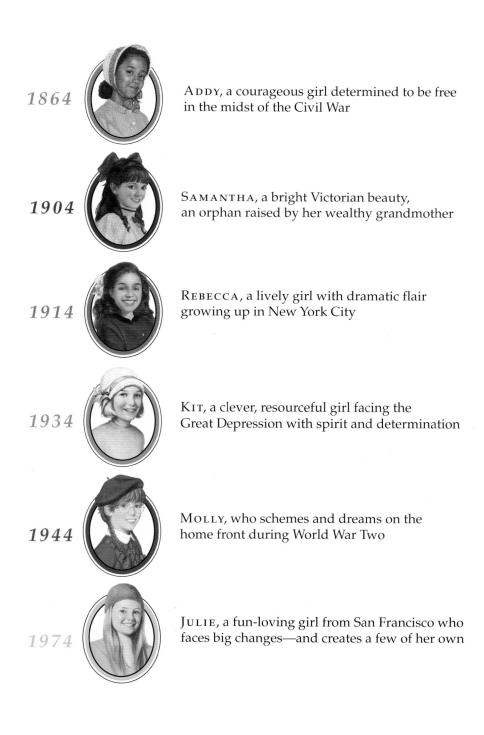

1864 ADDY, a courageous girl determined to be free in the midst of the Civil War

1904 SAMANTHA, a bright Victorian beauty, an orphan raised by her wealthy grandmother

1914 REBECCA, a lively girl with dramatic flair growing up in New York City

1934 KIT, a clever, resourceful girl facing the Great Depression with spirit and determination

1944 MOLLY, who schemes and dreams on the home front during World War Two

1974 JULIE, a fun-loving girl from San Francisco who faces big changes—and creates a few of her own

Questions or comments? Call 1-800-845-0005, visit **americangirl.com**,
or write to Customer Service, American Girl, 8400 Fairway Place,
Middleton, WI 53562-0497.

Printed in China
11 12 13 14 15 16 17 LEO 10 9 8 7 6 5 4 3 2 1

Profound appreciation to Mary Niall Mitchell, Associate Professor of History, University of
New Orleans; Sally Kittredge Reeves, former Notarial Archivist, New Orleans; and
Thomas A. Klingler, Associate Professor, Department of French and Italian, Tulane University

PICTURE CREDITS
The following individuals and organizations have generously
given permission to reprint images contained in "Looking Back":
p. 75—The Roger Ogden Collection from The Ogden Museum of Southern Art, University
of New Orleans in association with the Smithsonian Institution; p. 76—North Wind Picture
Archives; p. 77—Photograph provided by the Children's Aid Society (mother and child);
Ursuline Convent Archives (building); p. 78—© Bettmann/Corbis; p. 80—North Wind
Picture Archives; p. 81—Sisters of the Holy Family Archives

Cataloging-in-Publication Data available from the Library of Congress

FOR ALEXANDRA AND JESSICA

In 1853, many people in New Orleans spoke French as well as English. You'll see some French words in this book. For help in pronouncing or understanding the foreign words, look in the glossary beginning on page 82.

Table of Contents

Marie-Grace's Family and Friends

Marie-Grace's Family

PAPA
*Marie-Grace's father, a
dedicated doctor who is
serious but kind*

MRS. CURTIS
*A no-nonsense widow who
has been the Gardners'
housekeeper for four years*

MARIE-GRACE
*A shy, caring girl who
is happy to be back in
New Orleans*

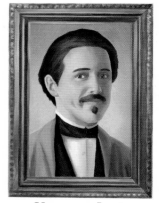

UNCLE LUC
*Marie-Grace's uncle, who
is a Mississippi River
steamboat pilot*

ARGOS
*Marie-Grace's dog, who is
her constant companion*

MADEMOISELLE OCÉANE
A French opera singer who gives voice lessons

CÉCILE REY
A confident girl who is Marie-Grace's first real friend

LAVINIA
A wealthy girl who likes to be the boss

SISTER BEATRICE
A warm and wise nun who is in charge at Holy Trinity Orphanage

Chapter One

A KNOCK AT NIGHT

May 1853
As Marie-Grace Gardner copied
out her French lesson, light from
the oil lamp glimmered off the
glass medicine bottles in her father's office. The
room was quiet. Even though it was late, her father,
Dr. Thaddeus Gardner, was still out seeing patients.

Marie-Grace could hardly wait for Papa to return
so that she could tell him her good news. A girl named
Isabelle had joined her class today. Marie-Grace
was usually shy. But she knew how hard it was to
be the new girl in school, so she had worked up her
courage and talked to Isabelle. The two of them had
sat together at lunch, and Marie-Grace had been

delighted to discover that Isabelle was quite friendly.

So far, Marie-Grace's only true friend in New Orleans was Cécile Rey. But Cécile and Marie-Grace did not go to school together. They usually only saw each other on Saturdays, when they both took singing lessons at the Royal Music Hall. *It would be nice to have a friend at school,* thought Marie-Grace, smiling. *Maybe Isabelle and I could play together after classes.*

As Marie-Grace dipped her pen in the inkwell, she remembered that she had bad news to share with her father, too. During supper, their new maid, Annie, had argued with their housekeeper, Mrs. Curtis. Annie had announced that she was quitting, and she'd left before the dishes were washed. Mrs. Curtis had gone to bed early with a headache.

Now Marie-Grace was the only one in the household who was awake. As she struggled with her French verbs, she listened for the sound of her father's key in the lock. But besides the scratching of her steel pen on the paper, all Marie-Grace could hear was the clock ticking and rain gently tapping on the front window.

Suddenly, a loud knock broke the silence. Marie-Grace was so startled that her hand jumped, leaving a heart-shaped ink spill on the page. Her dog, Argos, raced to the door, barking.

Marie-Grace knew that she should not unlock the door at night. If anyone came to the office after dark, Annie or Mrs. Curtis was supposed to answer the door. But Annie was gone, and Mrs. Curtis was asleep. So Marie-Grace blotted the ink stain and hoped that whoever was at the door would go away.

Then another knock sounded, even louder than the first. Marie-Grace guessed that the visitor could see the lamplight and thought that Dr. Gardner was in his office. "The office is closed," she called above Argos's barking. Then she repeated in French, *"Le bureau est fermé."*

A woman's muffled voice made a short reply. It sounded like, "Please take . . ." Marie-Grace could not understand the last few words.

After a few moments, Argos stopped barking, but he stood at the door, whimpering. Marie-Grace went to the front window and peeked around the curtains. The streetlamp on the corner cast a dim light. Marie-Grace could see that the woman had gone away, but she had left a basket on the step.

That's what Argos is excited about, Marie-Grace

realized. Her father often took care of people who had no money, and sometimes they left food as payment. Grateful patients brought fresh fish or jars of homemade pickles and preserves. One farmer had even delivered a large smoked ham.

Argos whined impatiently. "All right," Marie-Grace whispered. "We'll see what it is."

She opened the door. A light rain was falling, and the air smelled like the muddy levees along the Mississippi River. Holding tight to Argos's collar, Marie-Grace leaned down to look at the basket. There was a lump of something inside, but it was covered by a cloth. Curious, Marie-Grace pushed aside the cloth. Then she gasped. She let go of Argos's collar and picked up the basket. Then she carefully lifted the cloth and looked again. There could be no mistake—a sleeping baby lay nestled inside the basket.

"Gracious sakes!" breathed Marie-Grace as she stared at the child. She looked up and down the street. At first, she didn't see anyone. Then she caught a glimpse of movement at the end of the block. A slender woman with a cloth tied around her head was standing half-hidden by a building. "Madame!"

There could be no mistake—a sleeping baby lay nestled inside the basket.

Marie-Grace called. "Is this your baby?"

Instead of answering, the woman disappeared around the corner. A fresh breeze blew down the street, bringing with it a sprinkling of rain. The baby shuddered and gave a soft cry in its sleep. Argos looked up at Marie-Grace questioningly.

Marie-Grace knew what she had to do. She carried the basket into her father's office and carefully set it on the desk. By the light of the oil lamp, she saw that damp ringlets of hair framed the baby's face. The child held its tiny fist to its mouth, and its eyes were scrunched closed. "Hello!" she whispered to the sleeping infant. "You didn't get rained on, did you?"

The baby was wearing a patched gown that looked as if it had been made from an old flour sack. Marie-Grace touched the cloth and the baby woke. The child's blue-gray eyes looked up at her anxiously, a thin line forming between its delicately arched eyebrows.

"Don't cry," Marie-Grace said, gently stroking the baby's cheek. As she leaned over the basket, she sniffed something that smelled like coconut. "You'll be all right now. My papa will be home soon, and—"

A stern voice interrupted her. "Marie-Grace, why

6

is the door open?" It was her father. She had not even heard him come into the office. As he took off his overcoat and hat, he began to lecture her. "I've told you a thousand times that you must keep the office locked when you're alone here at night."

"A woman knocked on the door, Papa," Marie-Grace explained. "She went away, but look what she left." Marie-Grace stepped aside so that her father could see the basket.

"Who's this?" he asked, his voice softening.

Marie-Grace explained how she had found the child. "The woman was standing on the corner watching when I picked up the basket. But she ran away when I called to her."

"I'll see if anyone's out there now," her father said. He hurried out the door, not even stopping to put on his hat and coat. The baby began to whimper. Marie-Grace gently rocked the basket until her father returned a few minutes later, his hair wet from the rain. "There's no one on the street," he reported. "The woman must have stayed just long enough to make sure you brought the baby inside."

"Why would she do that?" asked Marie-Grace, looking down at the tiny baby.

"Once in Pennsylvania, a man left a baby on my doorstep," said Dr. Gardner, wiping his glasses with a towel. "The mother had died, and since I'm a doctor, the man thought the baby would be safe with me. I've heard of similar things happening to doctors here in New Orleans, too."

Dr. Gardner put the towel over his shoulder, and then he took the baby out of the basket. "The woman who was on the corner—have you seen her before?"

Marie-Grace bit her lip, trying to remember what the woman had looked like. "I don't think so," she said at last. "But it was dark, and all I could tell was that she was thin." Marie-Grace thought for a moment. "She had a kerchief around her head, too, like the ones the women in the market wear."

Her father began to undress the baby, and suddenly Marie-Grace smelled something that wasn't coconut at all. Her father sighed. "We need to change him. Would you get me a few more towels?"

Marie-Grace ran upstairs. When she returned with an armful of towels, the baby was wailing pitifully. Her father wrapped the child in clean linen, and then he started mixing something in one of his medicine beakers.

"What's wrong?" Marie-Grace asked anxiously. "Is the baby sick?"

"No. He's just hungry," said her father. "He's a few weeks old and looks healthy, but he's thin. I'm mixing some sugar and water to tide him over for now. Then I'll ask Mrs. Lambert if she'll nurse him along with her own baby."

Marie-Grace nodded. Mrs. Lambert was a cheerful woman who lived nearby. She had a large family, and she earned money by cleaning and doing laundry for neighbors. *Mrs. Lambert wouldn't mind taking care of one more baby,* Marie-Grace thought.

Dr. Gardner dipped his finger into the water and then touched the baby's lips with his moistened finger. The child stopped crying and sucked eagerly at the sugar water.

"He *is* hungry!" Marie-Grace exclaimed. "How could his mother leave him like that?"

"Whoever the mother was, I'll wager that she didn't *want* to leave him," said Dr. Gardner as he dipped his finger into the water again. "Desperate times call for desperate measures."

"What does that mean?" Marie-Grace asked.

"It means that sometimes you have to do very hard things, even though you don't want to. His mother—or somebody—tried to take care of him. He has a rash, but someone put a salve made with coconut oil on it. And whoever left him on the doorstep made sure that he was brought inside."

Marie-Grace was puzzled. "But why did she give him up?"

"My guess is that his mother loved him very much. She may have died, like the mother in Pennsylvania did. Or the baby's mother might be alive but in terrible circumstances. She may have given him up so that he could have a better life," said Dr. Gardner as the baby continued to suck hungrily at his finger.

Papa explained that women of color in New Orleans often wore kerchiefs around their heads. So the woman Marie-Grace had seen was either a free person of color or a slave. "If the baby's mother was a slave, she may have taken this desperate measure to keep her child from growing up in slavery."

Slavery! thought Marie-Grace, and she felt a chill

go up her spine. The baby's skin was about the same color as her own. But in New Orleans, there were so many different shades of skin color that it was sometimes hard to tell who was white and who was a person of color.

Marie-Grace knew that many people of color in the city were free, including her friend, Cécile. Cécile's father owned his own business, and Cécile lived in an elegant home and dressed in the latest fashions. She had a private tutor, and a maid accompanied her to music lessons. But Marie-Grace also knew that many people of color were slaves. They labored long hours without pay, and they could be sold to someone else at any time.

"It would be terrible to be a slave," Marie-Grace said, gazing down at the baby.

"We don't know that his mother was a slave," her father cautioned. "We don't even know that she was a person of color. The woman who left him here might have been a family friend or servant. We may never know who the child's parents are."

Just then the baby stopped sucking and started to cry again. "But we do know that he's not happy," Dr. Gardner said. He held the baby against his shoulder and walked him around the office. The child cried even louder.

As Marie-Grace watched her father pace the room, she recalled how he used to walk Daniel, her baby brother, in just the same way. She felt a twist in her stomach as she thought about her mother and brother, who had both died in a cholera epidemic more than four years ago. She remembered listening to the lullabies her mother sang to Daniel and hearing the thud of her father's footsteps in the hall as he walked Daniel for hours at a time.

"May I try?" Marie-Grace asked her father. He nodded and gently handed her the wailing infant. *"Fais dodo, mon enfant,"* Marie-Grace sang. "Go to sleep, my baby." She gently patted the baby on the back the way she remembered her mother soothing Daniel. The baby's sobs quieted. Then he nestled into her shoulder and closed his eyes.

"Good work," her father said. He lifted the sleeping baby out of her arms and tucked him back into his basket, covering him with a clean towel. Asleep, the baby looked like a perfect angel.

"Please, Papa, can he stay here with us?" Marie-Grace whispered to her father.

"No indeed," he said. "A baby needs a great deal of care. And we've lots to do already, don't we?"

She nodded reluctantly. She knew Papa was busy. After her mother and Daniel had died, Marie-Grace and her father had left New Orleans and lived in several small towns in the Northeast. They had returned to New Orleans just five months ago, and since then Papa had been working hard to build his medical practice.

"The warmest months are when diseases spread most quickly," her father reminded her. "So I'll be even busier with patients. I'm sure that Mrs. Curtis does not want a baby to take care of either, even with Annie's help."

Marie-Grace bit her lip. In all the excitement, she had forgotten to tell her father that Annie had quit. She quickly gave him the bad news. Papa sighed and said he would have to hire someone else to help with the housework.

Marie-Grace looked up at him. "But the baby can stay for a while, can't he?"

"A short while," her father said. "I'll put a notice about the baby in the newspaper. If his mother doesn't come to claim him, we'll take him to an orphanage where the nuns will care for him."

If they could not keep the baby at home, then an orphanage would be the next best choice, Marie-Grace decided. There was one across the street from her school, and she could visit him there. *It will be almost like having a little brother again,* she thought with a surge of happiness. *And someday I'll tell him how I found him in the rain and brought him into the house myself.*

Her father's voice broke into her thoughts. "While the baby is here, there will be more work for everyone," he warned. He looked at her over the top of his wire-rim glasses. "Will you help Mrs. Curtis?"

For a moment, Marie-Grace thought of the new girl at school. But playing with Isabelle could wait. "I'll come right home every day," she said.

"Good," said Papa, and he began to gather up the towels.

Marie-Grace leaned over the sleeping baby. "Don't worry," she whispered to him. "I'll take care of you. I promise."

HELP!

Marie-Grace decided to name the baby Philip because she had found him on St. Philip Street. "Doesn't 'Philip Gardner' sound nice?" she asked her father the next day.

"The baby is not a member of our family," her father reminded her. "He's only staying with us for a short time."

"But we can still call him Philip, can't we, Papa?" she persisted.

Papa nodded, a small smile on his lips. "Yes, Grace, I suppose we can call him Philip."

"Philip? More like Filled-up-with-Trouble!" snorted Mrs. Curtis. "As if I didn't have enough work to do, now we have another charity case to take care of!"

Over the next few days, Mrs. Curtis continued to complain about how much extra work the baby was. But Marie-Grace noticed that the housekeeper often smiled at Philip, and sometimes she even rocked him to sleep. Papa arranged for Mrs. Lambert to nurse Philip and assist Mrs. Curtis with the housework. Every day, Marie-Grace hurried home from school to help with Philip, too.

On Thursday afternoon, Marie-Grace found Mrs. Lambert hanging laundry to dry in the courtyard. Philip was lying in his basket in the shade of a tree. Argos sat nearby, keeping guard over the baby. The afternoon was warm, so Marie-Grace pulled a wide leaf from a palm tree and used it to gently fan Philip's face. He gurgled, as if tickled by the breeze. Marie-Grace picked him up carefully, just the way Mrs. Lambert had shown her. His head felt soft nestled in her arms. *This is just like having a little brother again*, she thought happily. She wished with all her heart that he could stay with her forever.

As she carried Philip around the courtyard, Marie-Grace showed him the flowers that bloomed by the walls. "Look, Philip—here's a yellow one," she told him, picking a bright blossom off a vine and holding it up for him to see. Philip, his dark curls damp with sweat, stared at the flower with wide eyes. "And here's a red one," she said, showing him a sweet-smelling rose.

"I do believe he likes flowers," Mrs. Lambert laughed. "But take care he doesn't touch them. I don't want him to put them in his mouth."

"I'll be very careful," Marie-Grace promised. She was showing Philip a lime tree when she heard a child crying. A few moments later, her father called from his office door, "Marie-Grace, would you assist me, please?"

"Yes, Papa," Marie-Grace answered. Her father often needed her to fetch supplies or hold his instruments as he stitched a patient's wounds. She put Philip back into his basket and hurried toward the office door.

A slender woman sat on the bench just outside the door, fanning her pale face. When Marie-Grace entered the room, she saw a blond girl, about four years old, perched on top of the examining table. The child was sniffling and her face was wet with tears.

Dr. Gardner beckoned to Marie-Grace.

"Susannah has a nasty splinter in her foot, and she won't keep still," he explained in a low voice. "I asked her mother to keep her calm, but Mrs. Stewart nearly fainted when I took out my instruments. Now Mrs. Stewart is waiting outside, so I need your help."

"I'll try," said Marie-Grace. She took a deep breath. She'd never had to calm a frightened child before. That was always the parent's job.

"We just have to get Susannah to think of something other than her foot. If we do, I'll have that splinter out in a twinkling."

Marie-Grace followed her father over to the examining table. "Now, Susannah," Dr. Gardner said patiently. "Your mother says you know your ABCs. Can you recite them for us?"

Susannah sniffled again and shook her head. "I don't know them now," she whispered.

Marie-Grace smiled sympathetically. Sometimes, when people stared at her and asked her questions, she couldn't remember anything, either.

Dr. Gardner sighed. "Well, I just need to look at that splinter," he said.

But when he picked up his magnifying glass, Susannah kicked wildly and screamed, "No! No!"

She did not stop screaming until he put down the magnifying glass.

Marie-Grace suddenly had an idea. "I know a song," she told Susannah. "It's called 'Twinkle, Twinkle, Little Star'."

Susannah turned to her. "I know it, too," she said, her lower lip still quivering.

"Really?" asked Marie-Grace, pretending to be surprised. "If you can sing the whole song, I'll give you one of those sweets." She pointed to a jar on the shelf.

Susannah's eyes widened when she saw the candy. She took a deep breath and began to sing, "Twinkle, twinkle—" But as soon as she saw Dr. Gardner pick up his metal tweezers, she screamed and pulled her foot away.

"Don't look at your foot. Hold my hand and look at me," said Marie-Grace, moving to block Susannah's view of the tweezers. "We'll sing together."

Marie-Grace's music teacher, Mademoiselle Océane, had taught her how to sing powerfully. Now Marie-Grace sang out with all her strength. She squeezed Susannah's hand, and the little girl joined in. As they sang together, "Like a diamond in the sky,"

Dr. Gardner held up a sliver of wood almost an inch long.

"Finished," he announced.

"You sang very well, Susannah!" exclaimed Marie-Grace, hurrying to fetch the jar of sweets.

Susannah smiled as she picked out a peppermint stick. As soon as she tasted it, she seemed to forget all about her splinter. She sat quietly while Dr. Gardner put a bandage on her foot. A few minutes later, she was holding her mother's hand and walking down the sidewalk as if her foot had never bothered her in the slightest.

"I'm glad that's over," Marie-Grace confessed to her father when they were alone in the examination room. "When Susannah cried, I wanted to cry along with her."

Her father was putting his magnifying glass back in its leather case. "You stayed calm, and you did what was best for Susannah. If we'd left that splinter in her foot, she might have developed a more serious problem. So it's good that we acted quickly." He looked at Marie-Grace. "Thank you for being my assistant."

Papa called me his assistant, thought Marie-Grace.

And I helped Susannah! She felt a glow of pride as she helped her father put away the supplies. Marie-Grace made sure that everything was in its proper place, just as a good assistant should. *If Papa needs my help again, I'll be ready,* Marie-Grace told herself as the bell over the front door rang.

CHAPTER
THREE
—

PHILIP'S FUTURE

A moment later, Mrs. Curtis appeared in the doorway of the examining room. "A gentleman is here to see you, Dr. Gardner," she said with a disapproving air.

Dr. Gardner wiped his hands on a towel. "Thank you for your help, Grace. You can go back outside now," he said. Then he turned to the housekeeper. "Please show the patient in."

"He's not a patient, sir," said Mrs. Curtis, frowning. "He's come about the baby."

Marie-Grace froze. "He's here for Philip?"

Mrs. Curtis pursed her lips. "That's what he says."

"I see," said Dr. Gardner thoughtfully. He

straightened his jacket. "Well, I'd better go talk to him."

Marie-Grace followed her father to the door of his office. A burly man stood by Papa's desk. The man took off his hat and introduced himself as Carson Hearst, manager of the Rigby Plantation just outside New Orleans. "I saw in the newspaper that you found a baby, and I've come to claim him," said Mr. Hearst with an oily smile. "I have good reason to believe that the child is the rightful property of my employer."

Rightful property. The words echoed in Marie-Grace's head. *This man is saying that Philip is a slave,* she thought.

"That's impossible!" Marie-Grace exclaimed.

Her father looked surprised by her outburst. He glanced at her over his wire-rim glasses, as if warning her to be quiet.

Mr. Hearst smiled at Marie-Grace, showing his yellow teeth. "It's not impossible at all, young lady," he said. "A slave ran away a few weeks ago. She'd just given birth, and she took her baby with her. But it's likely she had to give up the boy to avoid detection."

"Why do you assume this is your slave's baby?" Dr. Gardner asked, stepping behind his desk. "I don't even know that he's a child of color."

"I've been talking to people hereabouts, and they say the baby you found is about a month old and light-skinned with dark hair," said Mr. Hearst. "Well, that's the right age for the child, and the mother is real light-skinned, too. So it's more than likely her child. All I want is to see that the baby is returned to his rightful owner."

Marie-Grace wanted to run to the courtyard and hide Philip so that Mr. Hearst could never find him. But her feet seemed fixed to the ground. She watched her father casually start to shuffle through his papers.

"Have you found the mother?" Dr. Gardner inquired. He sounded mildly curious.

Mr. Hearst admitted that he hadn't. "But we won't stop looking for either of them till we do," he promised. "They can't have gone too far."

"Well, you can have the child if you want him," Dr. Gardner said. "I've been hoping someone would turn up to pay his medical bill."

Marie-Grace watched in horror as her father pulled out a piece of paper and began to write a list of numbers. *Papa wouldn't really give Philip away, would he?* she wondered as her stomach tightened with fear.

Mr. Hearst raised his eyebrows. "Medical bill?"

"Why, if you've been asking around, you surely know that the child has been quite sickly," said Dr. Gardner, writing quickly. "I've done my best to get him stronger. I even hired a nurse for him. But he's weaker than a runt puppy, and I can't guarantee he'll survive much longer. Still, I deserve to be paid for all my work, don't you agree?" He put down his pen and handed Mr. Hearst the bill.

Mr. Hearst looked at the paper, and his face turned red. "You want this much money for taking care of a slave baby?" he demanded.

Dr. Gardner's eyes were suddenly steely. "I've detailed every expense, and I won't settle for a penny less. If you want to take the baby, you'll have to pay my bill first."

Mr. Hearst threw the paper on the desk. "That's highway robbery! And I only have your word that the baby is sick at all!" Mr. Hearst jammed his hat back on his head. "I'm going to keep looking till I find the baby—and his mother, too. Good day to you, sir!" he said. Then he stalked out of the office, slamming the door behind him.

As soon as Mr. Hearst was gone, Marie-Grace rushed over to her father. "You don't think Philip is going to die, do you, Papa?" she asked, gripping the desk tightly.

"Of course not," said her father. He tossed the bill into his desk drawer and smiled at Marie-Grace. "Philip has gained weight nicely, and his cheeks are almost chubby now. I think he'll be fine."

"Would you really have given Philip to that awful man?" she asked, searching her father's eyes. "Even if he'd had the money to pay your bill?"

He gave her shoulder a reassuring squeeze. "No indeed, Grace," he said. "But money is the one thing that people like Mr. Hearst understand. That's why I asked for so much. I knew Mr. Hearst would never pay it."

Marie-Grace relaxed her hold on the desk. "Do you think Mr. Hearst will come back?" she asked.

"He might," her father replied frowning. "Mr. Hearst seems to have made up his mind that Philip belongs to the Rigby plantation, and he may go to great lengths to claim him." Papa closed the desk drawer firmly. "I think it's time we take Philip to Holy Trinity," he continued. "Mr. Hearst won't look there since it's an orphanage for white children. As long as there's no problem with Father Sebastian,

Philip will be safe."

"Why would there be a problem?" asked Marie-Grace, frowning.

"The priest decides whether a child should be admitted to the orphanage," Papa said. "If Father Sebastian thinks that Philip might be a child of color, he could not allow him into Holy Trinity."

"Then what would happen to Philip?"

"Well, we would have to take him to another orphanage—perhaps one for children of color," Papa said.

"But Mr. Hearst might look for him there!" Marie-Grace protested.

"Don't worry about that now," said her father as he straightened his papers. "I'll tell the nuns at Holy Trinity that we'll bring Philip next week, and we'll see what happens then."

A chill ran up Marie-Grace's spine. *What will we do if Father Sebastian turns Philip away?* she worried.

"In the meantime," her father continued, "I need some things from Monsieur Dupont's pharmacy. Would you like to come with me?"

The pharmacy was in a small building tucked around the corner from Jackson Square. The shop was filled with colored bottles of medicines, all labeled with strange-sounding names. Marie-Grace usually liked to look around the pharmacy while her father talked with Monsieur Dupont, but today she was too worried to stay inside.

Instead, she took Argos for a walk through the gardens in Jackson Square. The square was busy,  with strolling couples admiring the flowers and street vendors selling their wares. Yet Marie-Grace hardly noticed the people around her. All she could think about was baby Philip and the terrible possibility that Mr. Hearst might claim him as a slave.

When she and Argos reached the far end of the square, Marie-Grace stopped to admire the magnificent St. Louis Cathedral. Looking up at the cross on top of the tallest center spire, Marie-Grace made a silent promise that she would do everything she could do to help Philip. *But what?* she wondered.

She was about to return to the pharmacy when

she saw a girl step outside through the cathedral's wide doors. With a jolt of surprise, Marie-Grace realized that it was Cécile. Her friend always looked elegant, but today she was wearing an especially beautiful dress, and she was talking to a handsome young man with a mustache.

Could that be her brother, Armand? Marie-Grace wondered. Cécile had often talked about her brother, but Marie-Grace didn't know what Armand looked like. She had never met any of Cécile's family. The Reys socialized mostly with other wealthy free people of color. Marie-Grace's father worked so much that he and Marie-Grace hardly socialized at all.

A few months ago, however, Marie-Grace and Cécile had both gone to Mardi Gras balls on the same evening. Their parties had been in separate ballrooms, just down the hall from each other, but Cécile had thought up a clever plan for the two girls to slip into each other's balls. She had dressed in a costume that was identical to Marie-Grace's. The girls had traded places and danced at each other's balls, and no one had discovered the switch.

Suddenly, Marie-Grace caught her breath. Thinking about the costumes had given her an idea that might save Philip. *If only I can get Cécile to help me,* she thought. But Cécile was busy talking with the young man, and Marie-Grace felt too shy to march over and interrupt their conversation. She stood watching her friend, uncertain what to do.

Argos started toward the cathedral, tugging at his leash. He looked back at Marie-Grace expectantly. "You're right," Marie-Grace whispered to the dog. "I have to try to tell her." Marie-Grace reached into her pocket. She had a stub of a pencil and an old shopping list. She tore off a corner of the paper and quickly scribbled a note to Cécile. *Can you meet me before lessons? It's important.* When she looked up, the young man was gone. *This is my chance,* thought Marie-Grace.

"Cécile!" she called as she and Argos ran up to cathedral together. "I'm so glad I saw you. I need your help."

Cécile looked concerned. "What's wrong?" she asked.

Marie-Grace was breathless. "I found—" she began. But before she could say anything more, the young man with the mustache came out of the cathedral with several other people. They were all

"I'm so glad I saw you," Marie-Grace said. *"I need your help."*

speaking French and laughing together.

"My brother has just returned from France," said Cécile, smiling. "Come, I'll introduce you to my family. "

Marie-Grace blushed. "Oh, no, I don't want to interrupt," she stammered. "I just wanted to give you this." She thrust the folded note toward Cécile.

Before Cécile could say anything, Marie-Grace and Argos ran back through the square. When she reached the edge of the gardens, Marie-Grace turned back to the cathedral. Her eyes met Cécile's, and Cécile nodded ever so slightly.

Marie-Grace's heart was pounding as she and Argos returned to Monsieur Dupont's pharmacy. *I hope Cécile can help me*, she thought. *Maybe together we can keep Philip safe from Mr. Hearst.*

A SECRET PLAN

On Saturday morning, a misty rain fell as Marie-Grace hurried to the Royal Music Hall. She tried to walk under the balconies that jutted over the sidewalks, but both she and Argos were damp when they arrived at the music hall's back entrance.

Louis, the building's watchman, opened the door for them. *"Bonjour,* Marie-Grace," he said cheerfully.

"Bonjour," Marie-Grace replied with a smile. Over the last few months, she and Argos had become friends with the elderly watchman. Every Saturday, Argos stayed with Louis while Marie-Grace went to her music lesson. Louis often gave treats to the dog, and this morning he had a special surprise for Argos.

"My wife wanted to use this in our soup, but I saved it for you, *mon ami*," said Louis as he handed Argos a meaty bone. Argos thudded his tail happily and settled down by Louis's chair.

Marie-Grace thanked Louis and patted Argos good-bye. Then she made her way down a long hall lined with portraits of famous musicians. She reached the grand entryway just as Cécile came in.

"What has happened?" Cécile asked the moment she saw Marie-Grace. There was concern in her voice, but her eyes were bright with curiosity.

A bearded man carrying a cello walked by and looked questioningly at the girls. "Let's go upstairs," Marie-Grace said. "I'll tell you everything."

The upstairs hall was deserted, and the two girls settled themselves on a chintz-covered bench outside Mademoiselle Océane's studio. As the rain drizzled against the window, Marie-Grace told her friend all about Philip.

"A baby!" Cécile gasped. "Someone left him on your doorstep? Oh, that poor little boy."

Marie-Grace nodded. "I brought him inside, and when I sang to him, he stopped crying."

"Well, babies cry a *lot*," Cécile said, pulling off

her white gloves. "I remember my little cousin René when he was a baby. He cried all the time."

"Philip hardly ever cries now," Marie-Grace said loyally, even though it was not exactly true. "But that's not the problem," she continued, her voice dropping to a whisper. "Philip is in danger. A man came looking for him." Marie-Grace told Cécile about Mr. Hearst's claim that Philip belonged to the Rigby Plantation.

Cécile's eyes widened. "Oh, no," she said. "Is the baby's mother a slave?"

"It's possible," Marie-Grace answered. She nervously twisted her skirt in her hands. "My papa says we may never know. He says we can't even be sure that the woman who left the baby with us was his mother."

"Is Mr. Hearst going to take Philip away?" Cécile asked anxiously.

"We can't let him!" exclaimed Marie-Grace. Her voice echoed in the empty hallway. She lowered it to a whisper again and said, "Philip would grow up as a slave."

Cécile shuddered. "The law says that if a baby's mother is a slave, then the baby is a slave, too. My grandfather says that the law isn't right. He says everyone deserves to be free." Her face was serious. "My family would never, ever keep slaves."

Marie-Grace nodded. "We have to help Philip," she said, her voice trembling. "Papa says we should take him to Holy Trinity Orphanage. It's for white children, so Mr. Hearst won't look for him there."

Cécile's face brightened. "My mother knows one of the nuns there. They will take good care of Philip."

"I hope so," said Marie-Grace, staring down at the floor. "First we have to get him *into* Holy Trinity. If the priest thinks that Philip is a child of color, he couldn't let him in. So I've been thinking. Remember when we changed places at the Mardi Gras ball? Everyone looked at our costumes, not at us."

"I remember," said Cécile. She looked confused. "But what does that have to do with the baby?"

"The only clothes Philip has now are worn and patched," Marie-Grace said. "What if we dressed him up? If he was wearing the kind of clothes that babies in fancy carriages wear—"

"—then no one would guess that he might be a slave's baby!" Cécile finished for her.

36

"Exactly!" Marie-Grace agreed excitedly. "But I need your help. There are no fancy baby clothes at my house."

Cécile grinned. "My aunt has a trunk full of René's baby clothes. Some have beautiful lace. I'm sure she'd let me borrow some."

"Would you ask her?"

Cécile did not hesitate. "Of course."

Marie-Grace sighed with relief. "That would be wonderful," she exclaimed. "But remember, we can't tell anyone about this unless we're sure we can trust them. Otherwise, Philip . . ." Marie-Grace could not finish her sentence. The possibility of Mr. Hearst carrying Philip away was too terrible to even think about.

"I'll do whatever I can to help," Cécile said, and she squeezed Marie-Grace's arm reassuringly. Then she and Marie-Grace began to discuss what clothes would be best for Philip. They became so involved in their plan that they didn't even hear Mademoiselle Océane arrive.

"What are you two whispering about?" asked Mademoiselle with a smile.

Marie-Grace and Cécile shared a glance.

Mademoiselle Océane was more than a teacher. She was a friend who could be trusted. "It's very important," Marie-Grace said.

"Then let's go inside," Mademoiselle suggested. "We have a few minutes before it's time for your lesson, Cécile."

In the studio, the girls told Mademoiselle Océane all about Philip and their plan to get him into the orphanage.

"*Le pauvre petit!* The poor little one," exclaimed Mademoiselle. She thought for a moment, and then she said, "I think I have just the thing to help you."

Mademoiselle Océane went to the back of the studio where she kept her costume trunks and a sewing basket. She brought out several yards of finely woven cotton. The bright blue fabric reminded Marie-Grace of the sky on a summer's day. "This would make a very nice blanket for a baby, *non?*"

"Yes!" both girls agreed.

Mademoiselle cut a generous square of the cotton and gave Marie-Grace a needle and thread. "You can hem the blanket while Cécile has her lesson."

The next hour passed quickly for Marie-Grace.

Outside, the rain stopped and the sun broke through the clouds. Inside, Marie-Grace sat by the window and happily sewed her best stitches. She liked listening to Mademoiselle Océane and Cécile sing together, and sometimes they invited her to join in on the chorus of a song.

Ever since her mother and brother had died, Marie-Grace had often felt lonely, especially when her father worked long hours. Now, with her teacher and her friend, she felt as if she were part of a happy family. *If we can get Philip into Holy Trinity,* she thought, *he'll be safe—and I can visit him and play with him. It will almost be like having a brother again.*

When Cécile's lesson was finished, Mademoiselle Océane admired Marie-Grace's careful stitching, and Cécile ran her hand over the silky smooth fabric. "This is such pretty material," Cécile exclaimed. "You could use it to make something for a *trousseau.*"

Marie-Grace was puzzled. "What's a trousseau?"

"It is what we in France call the linens and gowns that a young lady sews before she is married," explained Mademoiselle Océane, her eyes shining.

"Oh," said Marie-Grace. Then a thought suddenly

occurred to her. "Are you sewing *your* trousseau, Mademoiselle?"

Before Mademoiselle Océane could answer, Cécile blurted out, "Are you getting married soon, Mademoiselle?"

"*Oui!* Yes! Well, I hope so," Mademoiselle stammered. Smiling, she turned to Marie-Grace. "Your Uncle Luc has proposed!"

Marie-Grace was so surprised that she dropped her sewing needle. Together, she and Cécile peppered Mademoiselle with questions.

"Did you accept?" Marie-Grace asked.

"When is the wedding?" Cécile added.

"Calm yourselves," said Mademoiselle Océane, laughing. "First, let's have tea." She poured steaming tea into delicate china cups and put out a plate of crisp cookies. Then, as they sat together in the sunny studio, she explained that Marie-Grace's uncle, Luc Rousseau, had proposed two weeks ago.

Mademoiselle had said yes, and he had written to her father in France asking for permission.

"Once my papa has approved—and I am sure he

will—we will have a wedding in the cathedral, and you girls will be invited," Mademoiselle promised. She added that after the wedding, she and Monsieur Rousseau planned to travel by steamboat to the little town of Belle Chênière, not far from New Orleans, to visit the whole Rousseau family. "You and your papa should come along," she urged Marie-Grace. "They are your family, too."

"I would like that very much!" Marie-Grace said excitedly. Uncle Luc was her mother's brother, and he and Mama had grown up in Belle Chênière. As Marie-Grace picked up her needle to finish hemming the blanket, she thought about how wonderful it would be to visit her relatives with Uncle Luc and his new bride.

"A wedding," Cécile sighed with happiness. "I love weddings—and you will make a beautiful bride, Mademoiselle. I can hardly wait."

"*Merci,*" said Mademoiselle. "Thank you. But we must be patient. It will take several weeks before we get my father's reply from France, so the wedding will not be until late summer."

Cécile frowned. "Oh, Mademoiselle, you should not get married in the summer."

"Why ever not?" asked Mademoiselle.

"It gets very hot, so lots of people leave New Orleans," Cécile warned. "Some people go away because they are afraid of getting sick." She shook her head. "It would not be a good time for a wedding."

Marie-Grace looked up from her sewing. She'd heard about wealthy people spending the summer in the country or along the Mississippi River where it was cooler. But it hadn't occurred to her that Cécile or Mademoiselle Océane might go away, too. "Does *your* family leave?" she asked Cécile, dreading the answer.

"No," Cécile replied. "It's different for us. My papa has his business here, so we stay. Besides, we've lived in New Orleans all our lives. We are not so likely to get sick. But for newcomers, it's different."

"I'm not going to leave either," said Mademoiselle Océane firmly. "I've been in New Orleans since last October. I'm hardly a newcomer, and I don't mind heat, either. Monsieur Rousseau and I will live here throughout the year, so there's no reason we shouldn't get married in the summer."

Marie-Grace smiled with relief and made another stitch. She could hardly wait for Mademoiselle

Océane and Uncle Luc to be married. *She will be my aunt then*, Marie-Grace thought, as she pulled the thread through the fabric. *Then we'll truly be family!*

On Wednesday afternoon, a line of patients gathered outside Dr. Gardner's office. There was a man with broken ribs, a woman who had burned herself while cooking, and a child with a bad cough.

"I'm sorry, Grace," said Papa as he paused between patients. "I won't be able to go with you to the orphanage. You and Mrs. Lambert will have to take Philip. You'd better leave soon."

"We will, Papa. Very soon," said Marie-Grace, watching the street through the office window. Ever since she'd come home from school, she'd been waiting for Cécile to arrive with the baby clothes. *Where can Cécile be?* she wondered.

Marie-Grace went out to the courtyard. Mrs. Lambert had just bathed Philip with sweet-smelling soap, and now she was putting him in a clean diaper. Philip was howling in protest.

"I thought you said he never cried," said a

familiar voice. Marie-Grace turned and saw Cécile standing by the courtyard gate. The Reys' maid, Ellen, stood by a carriage in the street behind her.

"Thank heavens you're here," said Marie-Grace, rushing over to her friend. "Were you able to get a baby gown?"

"Yes," said Cécile enthusiastically. "And my aunt says you can keep it." She opened a paper package, and inside was a carefully ironed white cotton gown trimmed with lace. "It has a bonnet, too," she added, pulling out a matching cap.

"Oh, they're perfect," exclaimed Marie-Grace, admiring the fine lace. "Come and meet Philip."

"I can only stay a moment," Cécile said, glancing back at the waiting carriage. Then she grinned at Marie-Grace. "But I can't wait to see him."

As the girls crossed the courtyard, Cécile looked at the patients lined up outside the office door. "Why are all those people here?" she asked.

"They're waiting for Papa," said Marie-Grace proudly. "He's a very good doctor. People come from all over New Orleans to see him."

Argos was resting in the shade next to Philip's basket. As the girls approached, he stood up and gave

Cécile a friendly nuzzle. Cécile wrinkled her nose at the dog's greeting, but she smiled as soon as she saw Philip. The baby had stopped crying, and he looked at Cécile with wide-eyed curiosity.

"He's so tiny!" Cécile exclaimed. "Hello, Philip," she whispered, gently touching his hand. Philip grabbed her finger and gurgled happily.

Both girls laughed. "I think he likes his name," Marie-Grace told her friend.

"Let's see if the clothes fit," Cécile suggested. Together the girls carefully dressed Philip in the lace-trimmed gown. "He looks beautiful," Cécile said.

"He looks like a little prince," agreed Marie-Grace. As she covered Philip with the blue blanket that she had hemmed, Marie-Grace felt a lump in her throat. She swallowed hard. "Thank you, Cécile," she said.

"Miss Cécile," Ellen called from the gate. "What will your Maman say if you are late to tea?"

"I have to go," Cécile said reluctantly. She touched Philip's cheek, and then she turned to Marie-Grace. "I'm sure the plan will work," she reassured her friend. "How could anyone turn away such a sweet baby?"

"I'm sure the plan will work," Cécile *reassured Marie-Grace.*
"How could anyone turn away such a sweet baby?"

As Cécile climbed into her carriage, Mrs. Lambert admired Philip. "I've seen a lot of babies, but I've never seen a prettier one," she said. "Those new clothes do him proud." Then Mrs. Lambert sighed. "I suppose we should go now, shouldn't we?"

Marie-Grace nodded sadly. She smoothed his curls and put on the bonnet. On the way to the orphanage, Marie-Grace and Mrs. Lambert took turns carrying Philip's basket. Argos followed close behind, his tail hanging low, as if he knew that Philip was going away.

When they arrived at Holy Trinity, a sturdy-looking nun with bright blue eyes bustled out to welcome them. She introduced herself as Sister Beatrice. "What a beautiful baby!" she said, smiling at Philip. "Come with me. I'll take you to see Father Sebastian. He's expecting you."

The nun led them through a large courtyard behind the building. Marie-Grace saw several small children laughing and shouting in a game of tag. She was relieved that the children looked happy and that Sister Beatrice seemed kind.

Sister Beatrice ushered them into a dark office where a priest sat behind a mahogany table. Father

Sebastian was an old man with a fringe of white hair around his bald head. He motioned for them to put the basket on the table. "So, this is the child who was left on Dr. Gardner's doorstep, eh?" he asked, glancing at Philip, who was asleep.

"Yes, Father," said Mrs. Lambert, smoothing Philip's blanket.

The priest turned to Marie-Grace. "Your father says you were the one who found him. Was there a note of any kind?"

"No, Father." Marie-Grace tried to answer calmly, but her voice squeaked.

Father Sebastian leaned over and peered at Philip. Marie-Grace was so nervous, she could barely breathe. *Please let him say yes,* she thought.

Finally, Father Sebastian looked up. "This baby should not be here," he said, shaking his head sadly.

There was a stunned silence in the small office. Marie-Grace felt her stomach flip-flop. "But he's an orphan!" she burst out.

"And he needs a home," added Mrs. Lambert, her face flushed. "Why shouldn't he be here, Father?"

"Because he is obviously from a wealthy family," the priest explained. "There must be a very sad story somewhere." He shook his head again. "But I will enter him in the ledger. What have you called him?"

"Philip," said Marie-Grace. As she watched Father Sebastian write the name in a heavy bound book, she felt her stomach twist again. She was relieved that the plan had worked. Philip was safe now. Mr. Hearst would not look for him at Holy Trinity. But she would miss Philip terribly. *Who will sing to him when he cries?* she wondered.

Sister Beatrice seemed to read Marie-Grace's thoughts. "Don't worry," she said, picking up the basket. "We'll take good care of Philip. You can visit him whenever you like. In fact, all the children enjoy having visitors."

"I'll be here tomorrow," Marie-Grace promised.

CHAPTER
FIVE

MARIE-THE-GREAT

As soon as school ended the next day, Marie-Grace hurried across the street to the orphanage. Sister Beatrice showed her the nursery. It was a long room with whitewashed walls and large windows. Philip had his own cradle in the far corner, and he was sleeping soundly.

"Philip likes it when people sing to him," Marie-Grace told the young nun who was watching over the babies.

"Does he?" the nun asked with a smile. "We'll remember that."

"And he likes flowers," Marie-Grace added.

The nun nodded. "We'll remember that, too."

Marie-Grace sat with Philip for a long time, rocking his cradle gently as he slept. When she returned to the sunny courtyard, Sister Beatrice introduced her to some of the other children, including a young boy named Charlie and a little girl named Katy.

"This is Marie-Grace," Sister Beatrice told them. "Perhaps she will play with you."

"Oh yes, play with us, Marie-Great!" said four-year-old Charlie, who spoke with a slight lisp.

Marie-Grace saw a jump rope lying on the ground. "How about tug-of-war?" she suggested. She held one end of the rope while Charlie and Katy held the other end. Marie-Grace pretended to pull her hardest, but she allowed the children to slowly pull her over to their side of the yard. Finally, they all collapsed together in a heap, laughing.

Katy tugged on her sleeve. "Play with us again, Marie-Great," she pleaded. So Marie-Grace organized a game of hide-and-seek.

When it was time for Marie-Grace to leave, Sister Beatrice called her aside. "The children enjoyed your visit, Marie-the-Great," she said with a smile. "You may come back often, if you'd like."

"I'd like that very much," exclaimed Marie-Grace. All the way home, she thought of songs she could sing to Philip and new games she could play with the other children on her next visit.

Marie-Grace began to visit the orphanage every Tuesday and Thursday after school. She loved to carry Philip around the courtyard, and she always made a special point to sing to him and show him the flowers in bloom. One day, when she was holding him in her arms, he gave her a tiny toothless smile. "Look, Sister Beatrice," Marie-Grace called excitedly. "Philip smiled!"

Sister Beatrice and several women who helped at Holy Trinity all crowded around Marie-Grace. Philip smiled again. Mrs. Finch, one of the wealthy volunteers, exclaimed, "Why, isn't he the most delightful baby you ever saw?"

He surely is, thought Marie-Grace.

When Philip napped, Marie-Grace played with the other children. She was the youngest volunteer at the orphanage and, unlike the older ladies, she was willing to run around the courtyard with the children, teach them dominoes and jacks, and make up new games.

"We like you because you play with us, Marie-the-Great," Charlie told her.

Many of the children spoke French with just a few English words mixed in, so Marie-Grace found her own French improving as she talked with them. She began to remember words and phrases her mother had spoken to her when she was small. Soon, Marie-Grace found herself switching between French and English without even noticing. "Bonjour! Hello!" she greeted the children when she arrived at the orphanage, and they all chatted together in a cheerful blend of languages.

As the weeks of June went by, each day seemed hotter than the last. In the mornings, the air was already warm when Marie-Grace crawled out from under the curtain of mosquito netting that surrounded her bed. By noon, the whole city was broiling in the sun. Sometimes there was a breeze at dusk. But sundown brought swarms of buzzing flies and clouds of mosquitoes. Marie-Grace got so many mosquito bites that Mrs. Curtis made her wear cotton gloves at night so that she wouldn't scratch her skin raw while she slept.

Mosquitoes and heat weren't the only problems. One evening, Papa returned from visiting Charity Hospital, and he told Marie-Grace that there were several patients who were sick with yellow fever.

The news frightened Marie-Grace. When she was three years old, a deadly wave of yellow fever had swept through New Orleans, and more than two thousand people had died. Marie-Grace and her father had both caught the fever that summer, but they had been lucky enough to recover. All Marie-Grace could remember about the illness was her mother singing to her and wiping her forehead with a cool cloth.

Now Marie-Grace thought of Cécile's warning to Mademoiselle Océane. "Do people leave New Orleans because they are afraid of getting sick?" she asked her father.

"Some people do," he answered. Papa took off his glasses and rubbed his eyes. "No one knows what causes yellow fever or how to prevent it," he explained. "All we know is that the fever comes almost every year during the hottest months. Some years, there are only a few cases. Other years, the fever is much more dangerous."

For a moment, Marie-Grace was silent. She remembered what Cécile had said about newcomers getting sick, and she asked her father if it was true.

He nodded. "Yellow fever can strike anyone who hasn't had it already. Most newcomers haven't had the fever, so they're the ones more likely to get sick. And these days, the city is crowded with newcomers."

"You don't think the fever will spread around the city, do you, Papa?" Marie-Grace asked anxiously.

"I surely hope not," he said. But Marie-Grace saw two deep lines of worry etched across his forehead.

At school, Marie-Grace discovered that many families were leaving town because of rumors about the fever. Several girls missed the last weeks of class. Isabelle, the new girl, left before the term ended.

"Her mama said it was too hot here, but I'll bet she was afraid of yellow fever," sniffed Lavinia, the bossiest girl in the class. "They've gone to spend the summer in the country."

Lavinia's friend Sophronia fanned herself. "I wish *I* were someplace cooler," Sophronia said. "My papa says we'll leave as soon as school is over."

"Well, *my* papa's not afraid and he says we're staying," Lavinia replied in her know-it-all way. "He reads the newspapers every day, and he says there are no reports of the fever. All the talk about it is just plain foolishness."

Listening to Lavinia's chatter, Marie-Grace felt a shiver run up her spine. *I wish all the talk of yellow fever* **were** *just foolishness,* she thought. *But Papa says it isn't.*

July brought some unexpected cooler weather— and lots and lots of rain. Marie-Grace and Argos had to slosh through puddles in the courtyard, and it was so wet that her dresses began to smell damp and musty. Marie-Grace had hoped the rain might wash away the threat of yellow fever, but Papa told her that more cases of the disease kept appearing.

Because school was out, Marie-Grace was able to visit the orphanage almost every day. One morning,

Sister Beatrice called her into her office. "I have some good news about Philip," the nun began.

Marie-Grace brightened. She had been wondering when Philip would say his first word. *Maybe he said "Marie-Grace,"* she thought hopefully.

But the news wasn't at all what she expected. Sister Beatrice told her that Mrs. Finch had become very fond of Philip. "He reminds her of one of her grandsons who passed away a few years ago," the nun explained. "She's become quite attached to Philip."

Marie-Grace smiled politely, but she wondered why this was especially good news. Anyone who knew Philip would be fond of him.

Sister Beatrice took a deep breath. "Mrs. Finch has decided to leave for the summer," she continued. "She's heard all the rumors about yellow fever, so she's going to stay with family in Illinois. She wants Philip to be safe from the fever, too, so she's offered to take him with her."

"She wants to take him away?" Marie-Grace blurted out. She felt as if the world were spinning around her. How could Sister Beatrice even suggest such a terrible thing?

"Mrs. Finch wants to take him to one of our sister convents in Chicago," the nun explained. "They have a fine orphanage there, and I know he will be well cared for. He's quite likely to be adopted."

I'd never see him again! thought Marie-Grace. Despair swelled up in her, and she stared at the ground, unable to say anything.

"Mrs. Finch's offer is very generous," Sister Beatrice continued. "Yet before I can allow Philip to leave, I must be sure that your father believes that the baby's mother will not return. Will you speak to your father for me and tell me his answer when you come back?"

Marie-Grace nodded. She felt a glimmer of hope. *Papa won't let anyone take Philip away,* she told herself. *All he has to do is say no, and Philip will stay here with us.*

That afternoon, Marie-Grace gave Sister Beatrice's message to her father at dinner. "We don't want Philip to go away, do we, Papa?" she asked as she passed him the bowl of gravy.

"Actually, it sounds like an excellent plan to me," said her father, and he spooned the gravy over his beefsteak and rice.

Marie-Grace stared at him. "But Philip is happy at Holy Trinity, and we can visit him whenever we want. Shouldn't he stay here in New Orleans?"

"At another time, I'd agree with you," her father said. He broke off a piece of French bread and dipped it into the rich gravy. "But because of yellow fever, Philip might be better off in Chicago.

"*We* aren't leaving New Orleans," Marie-Grace reminded her father. "Why should Philip have to go away?"

"Two important reasons," her father said. "First, Philip might get sick. You and I have already had yellow fever, so we won't get it again. But Philip has never had it. Second, Mr. Hearst isn't likely to go all the way to Chicago. So Philip would be safer there."

Marie-Grace wanted Philip to be safe, but she couldn't bear the thought of him being so far away. "You said Philip would be safe at Holy Trinity," she reminded her father. "And what about his mother? What if she comes back for him and he's gone?"

"I suppose it's still possible that Philip's mother might return," Dr. Gardner said between bites. "But in medicine, you prepare for the most likely outcome, not the most unlikely. And I think it's highly unlikely that his mother will come back to claim him after all this time. Really, the child would be better off in Chicago."

Marie-Grace pushed away her plate, unable to eat another bite. *I can't let Philip leave,* she thought. *I just can't!*

◈

When Marie-Grace returned to the orphanage the next day, she tried very hard to avoid Sister Beatrice. But Sister Beatrice found her when she was playing cards with Charlie and Katy. "Marie-the-Great," she said with a smile, "please come to my office as soon as your game is over."

When Marie-Grace appeared in the office doorway, Sister Beatrice looked up from her work. "Did you talk to your father about Philip?"

"Yes, Sister," Marie-Grace said slowly.

"What did he say?" Sister Beatrice asked.

Marie-Grace suddenly remembered her father's exact words. "He said, 'it's still possible that Philip's mother might return,'" she reported.

As soon as the words were out of her mouth,

Marie-Grace felt her face blush bright pink. *It's not exactly a lie,* she told herself. *Papa did say it was possible, just not likely.*

"I see," said Sister Beatrice, but she sounded disappointed. "Well, Mrs. Finch isn't leaving for a few days. Perhaps by the time she's ready to leave, your father will be ready to let Philip go with her."

"Perhaps," agreed Marie-Grace, but her eyes did not meet Sister Beatrice's.

CHAPTER
SIX

DESPERATE
MEASURES

On Saturday, Marie-Grace was
about to leave for her music lesson
when Mrs. Curtis stopped her in
the courtyard. "Here," said the housekeeper, handing
her a head of garlic tied to a long string. "Wear this.
It'll keep you from getting yellow fever."

It was a hot, sticky morning, and Marie-Grace
did not want to wear smelly garlic all day. "No, thank
you," she said, giving the string back to Mrs. Curtis.
"Papa told me that garlic won't keep away the fever. It
will just keep other people away. Besides, I've already
had the fever, and Papa says I won't get it again."

"Don't be too sure, missy. These days it's best
to do everything you can to protect yourself," said

Mrs. Curtis. The housekeeper already had garlic in the pockets of her apron and bags of cinnamon and nutmeg, too, for extra protection. The smell reminded Marie-Grace of the spice stalls at the French Market.

"I just heard that Mrs. Stewart down the street has taken sick with yellow fever," Mrs. Curtis continued as she hung the string of garlic around her own neck.

Marie-Grace paused. "Susannah's mother?" she asked in disbelief. It wasn't that long ago that she had helped Papa remove the splinter from Susannah's foot, and she often saw Susannah and her mother at the market.

"Yes, that's the one," said Mrs. Curtis. "Poor thing. They say she's very sick."

Marie-Grace remembered how frightened she had been when her own mother had been sick. Now her heart ached for Susannah—and her mother. "I hope Mrs. Stewart gets well," Marie-Grace said.

"I hope so, too," agreed Mrs. Curtis. "Your father is going to visit her this morning. But you stay away from anyone who looks sick."

"I will," Marie-Grace said solemnly. Then she and Argos hurried out of the courtyard.

On the way to the Royal Music Hall, Marie-Grace noticed how crowded the sidewalks were. Many of the people bustling by were dressed up and carrying luggage, as if they were going away. All the cabs were in use, too. Drivers sweated as they loaded trunks and crates onto their carriages, while the horses stomped and flicked their tails to swat away flies.

Marie-Grace was about to cross the street when a cab rumbled past and nearly hit Argos. Startled, Marie-Grace stepped back, pulling Argos to safety. She watched the carriage rush toward the Mississippi River. Along the levee, there were long lines of people waiting to board ships and steamboats. Marie-Grace wondered if all these people were leaving because of yellow fever.

"Be careful, mademoiselle!" warned a driver from another cab. "Everyone in the city is in a hurry hurry today, so you and your dog had better watch where you're going."

Marie-Grace held tightly to Argos's collar as they crossed the street. On the next block, she passed a house that belonged to a member of the Howard Association. Papa had told her all about the Howards. They were a group of brave volunteers who helped

"Be careful, mademoiselle!" warned a driver from another cab.

yellow fever victims, and
they saved the lives of
many people. Each Howard
member kept a slate outside
his home. On this slate,
someone had written a
message asking for help for
a family with two children
sick from the fever.

Marie-Grace knew that a Howard volunteer
would soon visit the Blanchard family and help them
get medicine, food, and any other care they needed,
all for free. Papa was one of the doctors that the
Howards relied on, and he had been working long
days and into the nights to treat the sick. Marie-Grace
was proud of her father—and proud to live in a city
where kind people worked so hard to help others.

*I don't think there's any better place in the world to
live than New Orleans,* she thought as she entered the
alley leading to the Royal Music Hall. *If only yellow
fever would go away—and if only it were just a little
cooler!*

As soon as she and Argos walked through the
back door of the music hall, Marie-Grace noticed

something different. Louis was not in his usual place. The watchman's stool was empty and the back entrance was deserted. Marie-Grace felt uneasy leaving Argos, and suddenly she did not want to be alone. "Come on, Argos," she said, and together they headed for Mademoiselle's studio.

Halfway up the staircase, Marie-Grace heard quick footsteps above her. She looked up, hoping it was Cécile. She was surprised to see Mademoiselle Océane instead. The singing teacher was wearing her bonnet and gloves, and she looked upset.

"Ah, Marie-Grace! I am glad to see you," Mademoiselle called down to her. "I just left a note for you. I'm sorry, but your lesson must wait for another day."

"Is something wrong?" Marie-Grace asked.

"Yes, very wrong," said Mademoiselle as she came quickly down the long staircase. "I just learned that my good friend Gabrielle is sick with yellow fever. She has no family here—I must get a cab and go see her. I will have the driver take you home, too."

Marie-Grace gripped the banister. It was Gabrielle who had helped arrange her invitation to the children's Mardi Gras ball. "I'm so sorry, Mademoiselle," she said, and she turned to follow her teacher down the stairs. Then Marie-Grace hesitated. She did not want to leave without seeing her friend. "Is Cécile still here?"

"No," said Mademoiselle, frowning. "I sent her home early so that I could go to Gabrielle."

Marie-Grace followed Mademoiselle out the back entrance. Louis's stool was still empty. "Where is Louis?" asked Marie-Grace as they walked through the shaded alley and out to the busy street.

"His granddaughter is sick with the fever," said Mademoiselle Océane as she waved to an approaching cab. "She is just a baby. Louis wasn't here yesterday, either."

Louis must be very worried, Marie-Grace thought as the cab stopped in front of them. With a heavy heart, she followed Mademoiselle into the carriage. Argos settled himself between them, and Marie-Grace hugged the dog, trying to reassure herself.

As they traveled through the busy streets, the carriage stopped to let a slow-moving funeral procession pass. Marie-Grace felt tears come to her eyes as she watched the mourners, bent over with grief, walking behind the coffin.

"Mademoiselle," Marie-Grace whispered, "do you think . . . is it yellow fever?"

"I do not know for certain," Mademoiselle Océane said hesitantly. "But yes, I think it may be." She took a deep breath. "Another singer at the opera—a very talented young man—became sick with the fever on Monday." Mademoiselle paused. "He died yesterday," she continued sadly. "That is why I am so worried about Gabrielle."

Just then the cab pulled up in front of a small house. Mademoiselle paid the driver and gave him extra money to take Marie-Grace home. Then she turned back to Marie-Grace and hugged her for a long moment. "Be brave, *chérie*," she said. "Our friends need us to be strong, even if it's not easy." Mademoiselle smiled. "And I will see you next week, *non?*"

"Yes," Marie-Grace said, and she forced herself to smile, too.

But as soon as she was alone in the carriage, Marie-Grace buried her head in Argos's soft fur. She did not want to look outside anymore. She did not want to see people hurrying out of the city. She did not want to see the names of the sick chalked on slates. Yellow fever no longer seemed to be a sickness that only affected other people. It threatened her neighbors and friends—anyone who had not already had the disease. And neither garlic nor anything else would protect them. *I wish I could do something to help,* Marie-Grace thought desperately.

When she finally looked up, she saw that the carriage was passing Holy Trinity. Suddenly, Marie-Grace knew what she could do. "Would you stop here, please?" she called to the driver.

There was a water trough for horses on the street just outside the orphanage, and Marie-Grace waited while Argos took a long drink. Then she left him under a shady tree in the courtyard and hurried to Sister Beatrice's office.

The nun was writing in a ledger book when Marie-Grace entered. "Excuse me, Sister," Marie-Grace began. Then she stopped, uncertain what to say next.

"Yes, Marie-the-Great?" the nun asked encouragingly. "Is there something bothering you?"

Suddenly, the words tumbled out. Marie-Grace told Sister Beatrice that her father had actually said it was a good idea for Philip to go to Chicago.

"I lied to you because I wanted Philip to stay here," Marie-Grace confessed.

She waited for Sister Beatrice to lecture her. Instead, the nun simply asked, "Why did you decide to tell the truth today?"

Marie-Grace hung her head. "I've been hearing about so many people who are sick, and I'm scared that Philip will get sick, too. I know I should have told you the truth before. I'm very sorry. But please, can Philip still go with Mrs. Finch?"

Sister Beatrice put down her pen. "Fortunately, you're not too late. Mrs. Finch is not leaving until tomorrow, and she's still willing to take Philip with her."

Marie-Grace felt weak with relief. "Do you think Philip will remember us?" she asked hopefully.

The nun shook her head. "No, I am afraid he won't. But he'll be safe. And in these difficult times, that's the most we can hope for."

"Yes, Sister," said Marie-Grace, but she felt a wave of sadness. *Philip will be gone tomorrow!* she realized.

Sister Beatrice's bright blue eyes studied Marie-Grace's face. "I know it will be hard for you to say good-bye to Philip," she added gently. "But you are doing what's best for him—and I'm proud of you for that." She glanced at the ledger in front of her. "We've just admitted thirteen children who were orphaned by the fever. I expect we will soon be receiving more." She looked at Marie-Grace. "I hope you'll continue to visit, even though Philip won't be here. The little ones are happy when you play with them, and we'll need your help now more than ever."

Marie-Grace nodded. "I'll come as often as I can."

"Good. Now let's go see Philip together," said Sister Beatrice. She gave Marie-Grace a sad smile. "I shall miss him, too."

They found Philip in his cradle. Two other babies were now in the nursery, and one of them was crying, but Philip slept peacefully through the noise. While Sister Beatrice comforted the crying child, Marie-Grace straightened the blue blanket she had hemmed for Philip. Tears slid down her cheeks as she realized that she would not be a big sister to him after all. She would never be able to tell him how she had rescued him from the rain, and she would not be there to see him grow up.

Marie-Grace leaned down and whispered to Philip. She tucked in his blanket one last time and, fighting back sobs, she made her way out of the nursery. She was hurrying through the courtyard when she felt a tug on her arm. It was Charlie. He had run to catch up with her. Katy was behind him, and they both looked up at her expectantly.

"Can you play hide-and-seek with us, Marie-the-Great?" Charlie asked.

"Please?" Katy added.

All Marie-Grace wanted was to go home with Argos and cry. She was about to tell Charlie and Katy that she could not play today when she remembered Mademoiselle's words. *Our friends need us to be strong, even if it's not easy.*

Marie-Grace wiped her eyes. "Of course I can play," she said, forcing a smile. "I'm Marie-the-Great! But you'd better hide quick!"

Giggling, the two children skipped off. Marie-Grace took a deep breath, and then she covered her eyes with her fingers and started to count down. "Ten, nine, eight..."

LOOKING BACK

ORPHANS IN AMERICA
1853

Marie-Grace couldn't believe someone would leave a baby on a stranger's doorstep. But in the 1800s, abandoned children were a part of life in America. Giving up a child was heart-breaking for many parents—but sometimes they had no choice.

CITY INTELLIGENCE.

CHILD FOUND.—A baker, whose name is not given, but who lives at the corner of Port and Rampart streets, reported last night at the police office of the Third District that he had found a child about three years old, who speaks German. Persons interested in the little foundling can obtain information by applying at the above mentioned locality.

*Like Philip, many children were left with doctors or at orphanages. Others were discovered by police. Newspapers, like this one from New Orleans, included notices about **foundlings**, or abandoned children.*

Many children became orphans when their fathers were injured or killed in workplace accidents. Mothers could not take care of their children and work at the same time. Without day-care centers, there was little help for working mothers who did not have family or friends nearby. The only thing some mothers could do to keep their children from starving was to take them to an orphanage. As Marie-Grace's father explained, these sorts of desperate circumstances forced people to make difficult decisions. Many parents chose to give up their children in the hopes that their sons and daughters would have better lives.

Poverty was not the only reason orphanages were necessary. Throughout the 1800s, children frequently lost one or both parents to diseases such as cholera *(KAH-ler-uh)*, smallpox, and yellow fever. When disease spreads quickly and affects large numbers of people, it's called an *epidemic*. From the 1830s through the 1860s, more than one hundred new orphanages were built across the country to care for children left alone by these devastating events. The need was especially great after the cholera epidemic of 1849—the same epidemic that took the lives of Marie-Grace's mother and baby brother.

Parents who had no place to live sometimes gave up their children to keep them warm and safe.

The Ursuline nuns ran one of the many orphanages in New Orleans. Across America, big cities had several orphanages to house all the children who needed care.

Most children in orphanages were "half orphans"—one of their parents was still alive. During epidemics, though, children were more likely to be "full orphans." That meant that neither parent was alive. Some children lost their entire families in an epidemic. Immigrant children were especially vulnerable to becoming full orphans. Their families were more likely to get sick because they usually lived in crowded areas of cities where diseases spread quickly. And they were more likely to die because they had not been exposed to the disease in their native countries. Like Philip, many children were orphaned at such a young age that they didn't even know their own names. They grew up without any information about their parents or their family background.

A nurse adds another name to a long list of orphaned children.

A fireworks display raised money for a New Orleans orphanage in 1853.

If children did not have family or friends who could adopt them, they usually went to orphanages that were operated by religious organizations. Protestant, Catholic, and Jewish groups built and ran orphanages and paid for the care of the children. But orphanages depended on the community for help, too. Local families organized annual collections and fund-raising events, including charity balls and even fireworks displays. In New Orleans, vendors from the French Market supplied the Camp Street Female Orphan Asylum with fresh vegetables and other food. In Cincinnati, merchants donated cloth and buttons so that neighbors could sew clothes for the orphans. And all around the country, people like Marie-Grace and Cécile volunteered their time to help children who were living without their parents.

In addition to providing food, clothing, and shelter, orphanages gave children a chance to learn. The first public schools in America were small and did not have room for all the children who lived nearby. Orphanages were often the only places poor children could get an education.

Margaret Haughery (HAW-ree) established several New Orleans orphanages. During the 1853 epidemic, she cared for many sick mothers, promising them that she would look after their children.

79

The busy dining room of the New York Colored Orphan Asylum

Daily life varied from one orphanage to the next. Some were like Holy Trinity, the fictional orphanage where Marie-Grace took Philip. Caregivers tried to make the orphanage feel like a home, and they gave children plenty of time to play. But other orphanages ran on a rigid schedule and had strict rules. Children slept, ate, and studied at the same time every day. When they weren't in school or at prayer, they were doing chores. Orphans swept floors, made beds, and mended clothes. Silence during meals was a common rule, and children had only one hour a day to play.

Many orphanages housed just girls or just boys, but almost all orphanages were for white children only. Until the 1860s, most black children in America lived in slavery. They were often separated from their parents when someone in the family was sold. Children were then raised by other slaves. But there were a few orphanages for free children of color. The New York Colored Orphan Asylum opened in 1836. Starting in the 1840s, a group of African American nuns called the Sisters of the Holy Family cared for orphaned girls of color in New Orleans.

Today, large orphanages are rare in America. Since the early 1900s, many agencies have been established to help families stay together or to find homes for children who need care. And thanks to better sanitation and health care, epidemics are less likely to leave thousands of children orphaned and alone.

By the 1900s, the Sisters of the Holy Family were educating girls of color in New Orleans, as well as caring for orphans.

GLOSSARY OF FRENCH WORDS

bonjour *(bohn-zhoor)*—hello

chérie *(shay-ree)*—dear, darling

Fais dodo, mon enfant. *(feh doh-doh, mohn ahn-fahn)*—Sleep, my baby. This is a line from a traditional lullaby.

Le bureau est fermé. *(luh byew-roh ay fehr-may)*—The office is closed.

Le pauvre petit! *(luh poh-vruh puh-tee)*—The poor little thing!

Madame *(mah-dahm)*—Mrs., ma'am

Mademoiselle *(mahd-mwah-zel)*—Miss

Mardi Gras *(mar-dee grah)*—A day of feasting and parties in February or March, 40 days before Easter

merci *(mehr-see)*—thank you

mon ami *(mohn ah-mee)*—my friend

Monsieur *(muh-syuh)*—Mr., sir

non *(nohn)*—no

oui *(wee)*—yes

trousseau *(troo-soh)*—the household linens and clothing that a young woman sews before her wedding, to use after she is married

How to Pronounce French Names

Armand *(ar-mahnd)*

Belle Chênière *(bel sheh-nyehr)*—a fictional village outside of New Orleans where Marie-Grace's relatives live. The name means "beautiful oak grove."

Cécile Rey *(say-seel ray)*

Dupont *(dew-pohn)*

Gabrielle *(gah-bree-el)*

Louis *(loo-ee)*

Luc Rousseau *(lewk roo-soh)*

Océane Michel *(oh-say-ahn mee-shel)*

Réne *(ruh-neh)*

GET THE WHOLE STORY

Two very different girls share a unique friendship and a remarkable story. Cécile's and Marie-Grace's books take turns describing the year that changes both their lives. Read all six!

Available at bookstores and at *americangirl.com*

BOOK 1: MEET MARIE-GRACE

When Marie-Grace arrives in New Orleans, she's not sure she fits in—until an unexpected invitation opens the door to friendship.

BOOK 2: MEET CÉCILE

Cécile plans a secret adventure at a glittering costume ball. But her daring plan won't work unless Marie-Grace is brave enough to take part, too!

BOOK 3: MARIE-GRACE AND THE ORPHANS

Marie-Grace discovers an abandoned baby. With Cécile's help, she finds a safe place for him. But when a fever threatens the city, she wonders if *anyone* will be safe.

BOOK 4: TROUBLES FOR CÉCILE

Yellow fever spreads through the city—and into Cécile's own home. Marie-Grace offers help, but it's up to Cécile to be strong when her family needs her most.

BOOK 5: MARIE-GRACE MAKES A DIFFERENCE

As the fever rages on, Marie-Grace and Cécile volunteer at a crowded orphanage. Then Marie-Grace discovers that it's not just the orphans who need help.

BOOK 6: CÉCILE'S GIFT

The epidemic is over, but it has changed Cécile—and New Orleans—forever. With Marie-Grace's encouragement, Cécile steps onstage to help her beloved city recover.

A SNEAK PEEK AT
THE NEXT BOOK IN THE SERIES

TROUBLES FOR
Cécile

Cécile skipped beside her brother and her little cousin, René, at the park on the shores of Lake Pontchartrain, just outside the city. The cool breeze off the water made the park perfect for a picnic under the trees, and everyone in the Rey household had come to enjoy it.

"How I did miss all this when I was away in France!" Armand swept his hat into the air with one long arm, and the picnic basket he was holding in the other hand swung dangerously.

"Didn't you picnic in Paris?" Cécile asked.

"Yes, but with only a hungry memory of Maman's watermelon pickles and Mathilde's tea cakes," he said, lowering the basket carefully, for those precious goodies were inside it. He knelt to check them.

Still smiling, Cécile squinted against the sun. "Look! Papa has already found a picnic spot," she said, pointing up ahead to where her father and Grand-père were spreading a blanket under a shady tree. Beside them, Maman was busy gesturing to their young housemaid, Ellen, and Tante Tay was helping Mathilde, the cook, unpack a basket. René scampered off to join the grown-ups.

Armand rose and shrugged as he adjusted his hat.

"Look, Papa has already found a picnic spot!" Cécile said.

"There seem to be plenty of good picnic spots left."

"You're right," Cécile said, looking around. Scattered here and there were other family groups and clusters of friends, and a train had just pulled to a stop to let its passengers spill out. But the popular park did seem quiet for such a beautiful Sunday afternoon.

"Where is everybody?" Cécile wondered out loud. Then her eyes met her brother's. "You don't think it's because of yellow fever, do you?"

"Now, Cécé." Armand shook his head and spoke in his big-brother tone. "Don't let your imagination carry you away. Lots of families leave New Orleans for the summer. You know that."

Cécile knew that very well. She thought of reminding Armand that she also knew arithmetic very well and that today she could count the number of families sprinkled in the park.

"Put it out of your mind," Armand told her. "We're here for fun. Look who's gotten off the train!"

Cécile turned to see Monette Bruiller waving. She grinned and waved back. Like Cécile, Monette didn't have sisters, so they always enjoyed each other's company.

Cécile ran to join her friend. "Monette! *Bonjour.*"

"Bonjour, Cécile. I'm so glad to see you!" Monette smiled brightly, and the two girls began to stroll arm in arm. Armand swerved around them, hurrying to deliver his picnic basket so that he could join the noisy clump of Bruiller brothers.

"I haven't seen your brother since he came back from Paris," Monette said. "He is *très gentil.* Very nice!"

Cécile made a face, and Monette laughed. "But he's so handsome—not skinny like my brothers!"

"*Shhh!* Don't tell him that," Cécile joked. Suddenly the boys let out a loud cheer and ran together toward an open area between the trees. "Look! What are they doing?"

"Oh, they're starting a *raquettes* game," Monette said, tucking her black braids underneath her bonnet.

"Armand says he played almost the same game in France. They call it *lacrosse*," Cécile told her. "Let's watch."

The girls wandered toward the open space, where the boys had already grabbed long sticks and had begun to chase a small leather ball. They bumped shoulders roughly as each boy tried to scoop the ball into the basketlike end of his stick, hoping to toss the ball toward the goal—a small square of canvas hanging from a large, lonely tree.

Shouts went up from the adults who had gathered to watch the game. *"Merveilleux!* Armand just scored," Cécile said, clapping her hands. "Who is that boy who tried to knock him down? Is it Agnès Metoyer's brother?"

Monette shook her head and turned away from the noisy onlookers. "Didn't you hear?" she asked. "Agnès and Fanny's family left town yesterday. They're going to their uncle's plantation upriver."

Cécile shrugged. "They usually go away when it gets too hot, don't they?"

Monette leaned closer. "The Valliens are gone, too, and so are the Christophes and the Manuels— and those families *never* go away. My papa says most of his American customers have left, too." She paused and looked at Cécile with worried eyes. "They're all leaving because they're afraid of yellow fever."

Cécile's heart thumped. "Monette, do you know more?"

"Les enfants, venez manger!" Madame Bruiller's voice called out. "Children, come eat!"

"I'm sorry, Cécile, that's all I've heard." Monette

squeezed Cécile's shoulder and dashed off to eat with her family.

Cécile dragged her feet slowly through the grass. She turned back toward the game, but it was breaking up as the Bruiller brothers left to join their family. Cécile looked at the players and the small crowd that had gathered. How many of them would still be around next Sunday? Would her newest friend, Marie-Grace, leave New Orleans, too?

Armand came up beside her, still breathless from the game. "What in the world are you frowning about?" he teased. "Didn't you see me score?"

"Nothing... I mean, yes!" Cécile looked up at her brother's laughing face. Everyone was crowding around him now, congratulating him. She wouldn't spoil his great day by saying that horrid word—*fever*.